# THIS BOOK IS NOT ABOUT DRAGONS

BY Shelley Moore Thomas

ILLUSTRATED BY Fred Koehler

There are

**NO**

**DRAGONS**

in this book.

Go ahead.
Turn the page.

See, I told you.

NO DRAGONS.

What?
You want to know
what that is?

There?
By that tree?
Oh. That.

That is **NOT A DRAGON**.
That is a . . .

rabbit.

Long ears. Puffy tail.

See? It is a rabbit.

**IT CAN'T BE A DRAGON** because, remember?

This book is **NOT ABOUT DRAGONS.**

And there are
**NOT ANY DRAGONS**
on this page, either.

Oh, that? Right there,
next to the house?

That is **NOT A DRAGON.**

That is a truck. Yes, a truck.

Notice the wheels? The doors?
The bumper? That is a truck.

It is **NOT**
**A DRAGON.**

I already told you.
This book is . . .

**NOT**
**ABOUT**
**DRAGONS.**

This page is **100% DRAGON FREE.**
And no, don't even think it!
Those things in the sky are
**NOT DRAGONS.** They are clouds.

See how weightless they are?
Airy and light? They are
definitely **NOT DRAGONS**.
That is because this book is . . .

**NOT ABOUT DRAGONS.**

NONE HERE.

That is a moose.

**NONE HERE.**

That is pizza.

And none here. That is a baby chick. See? Not a **SINGLE DRAGON** around here.

So, um, that's pretty much it.

**NO DRAGONS.**

What?
You want to turn the page?
Er . . . um . . . no, you don't.
Why?
Well, because there are
**NOT ANY DRAGONS**
there.
**ABSOLUTELY
NO DRAGONS.**

And if you turn the page, you are
just going to be looking for them,
trying to find them, but they are
not there because this book is . . .

# NOT ABOUT DRAGONS.

Period.

# NO . . .
## don't turn the page!

NOOOOOOOO!

I guess I am going to
have to change the title.

I hope you are happy.

To Mikey, Zena, Henry, Daisy, and Jimmy
—SMT

To Morgann, Jon, Kelsey, and Makenzie, who kept the ship
from sinking while I attempted to tame the dragons
—FK

Text copyright © 2016 by Shelley Moore Thomas
Illustrations copyright © 2016 by Fred Koehler
All rights reserved.
For information about permission to reproduce selections from this book, contact permissions@highlights.com.

Boyds Mills Press
An Imprint of Highlights
815 Church Street
Honesdale, Pennsylvania 18431

Printed in China
ISBN: 978-1-62979-168-5
Library of Congress Control Number: 2015958448

First edition
Design by Sara Gillingham Studio.
Production by Sue Cole.
The text of this book is set in Brandon Grotesque and Pyrotechnics.
The illustrations were created using crumpled paper and various incendiary devices including smoke bombs, firecrackers,
and blow torches. The resulting detritus was photographed and assembled digitally with digitally rendered drawings.
No mice or dragons were harmed in the making of this book.

10 9 8 7 6 5 4 3 2 1